KYLA
miss.behaves
as an
international super spy

written & illustrated by

kyla may

PSS!
PRICE STERN SLOAN

PRICE STERN SLOAN

Published by the Penguin Group

Penguin Group (USA) Inc., 375 Hudson Street, New York, New York 10014, U.S.A. · Penguin Group
(Canada), 90 Eglinton Avenue, Suite 700, Toronto, Ontario, Canada M4P 2Y3 (a division of Pearson
Penguin Canada Inc.) · Penguin Books Ltd, 80 Strand, London WC2R ORL, England · Penguin Ireland,
25 St Stephen's Green, Dublin 2, Ireland (a division of Penguin Books Ltd) · Penguin Group
(Australia), 250 Camberwell Road, Camberwell, Victoria 3124, Australia (a division of Pearson
Australia Group Pty Ltd) · Penguin Books India Pvt Ltd, 11 Community Centre, Panchsheel Park,
New Delhi – 110 017, India · Penguin Group (NZ), Cnr Airborne and Rosedale Roads, Albany,
Auckland 1310, New Zealand (a division of Pearson New Zealand Ltd) · Penguin Books (South
Africa) (Pty) Ltd, 24 Sturdee Avenue, Rosebank, Johannesburg 2196, South Africa

Penguin Books Ltd, Registered Offices: 80 Strand, London WC2R ORL, England

Copyright © 2006 by Kyla May Pty Ltd. All rights reserved. Published by Price Stern Sloan,
a division of Penguin Young Readers Group, 345 Hudson Street, New York, New York 10014.
PSS! is a registered trademark of Penguin Group (USA) Inc. Manufactured in China.

Library of Congress Cataloging-in-Publication Data

May, Kyla.
  Kyla May Miss. Behaves as an international super spy / written & illustrated by Kyla May.
    p. cm.
  Summary: When her arch rival's favorite bracelet disappears at school, Kyla May, the main
suspect, must clear her name by using her imagination to become an international super spy.
  ISBN 0-8431-1397-9 (pbk)
  (1. Imagination--Fiction. 2. Spies--Fiction. 3. Schools--Fiction.) I. Title.

PZ7.M4535Kyku 2006
(Fic)--dc22
                                                                    2005032898

10 9 8 7 6 5 4 3 2 1

HELLO!...GUESS WHO?

Yep, ME - KYLA MAY MISS. BEHAVES
the fantabulous "One & Only." & Introducing the

B AND-NEW & iMPROVED ME!

surely
I don't
need ANY
improvement.

Why do i need improvement, U ask? Well,
Mum & Dad always say
each day's a chance 2 "turn
over a new leaf." Having thought
long & hard 'bout this, i've
decided 2 swallow my pride &
befriend my no.1 archrival,
my nemesis — Bianca Boticelli.

C my
special
dictionary
@ back
of journal!

🌸🌸🌸🌸🌸🌸🌸🌸🌸🌸🌸🌸

From now on, i'm going 2 B kind,
understanding, generous &
supportive 2 Bianca.

As of 2day, Bianca Boticelli will B my friend!

Hmmm...just "think"...we could hang out?... ☺

Wonder if she likes hot chocolate as much as i do?

Go shopping together?...

Fifi-belle & Gemima could have play-dates!

Kyla May + Bianca were here!

Kyla May + Bianca friends 4eva!

4

Hmmm...even B school project partners?...

The possibilities R endless!
This will B fantabulous!!!

5

4get everything i just wrote!!!

Bianca is my worstest ENEMY EVER...& EVER X ∞ (times)

once again! i tell U...i have NO patience 4 (this is the "infinity symbol, which symbolizes 4ever... & ever & ever...nonstop)

Drama Queen

Miss. Drama Queen.

Drama, drama, drama!!!

She's absolutely impossible!
...i'm SOOOOOOOOOO over it!

Guess what just happened? ...Get ready 4 this –

U may need 2 sit down (if you're already sitting — lie down)!

OK, soooooo i went up 2 Bianca 2 make friends &

MISS. SHOW-OFFSKY

was, like, T☺TALLY showing off, as per usual (...like,
surprise, surprise)! This time over a new bracelet her
Daddy Dearest bought her. We just had gym class
& were all in the locker room changing from our
tennis outfits when Bianca yelled:

"Thief! Thief! Someone's stolen my bracelet!"

Like, PLEEEEEEEASE.
U'd think her bracelet
was...

The Crown Jewels!

Bianca's Bracelet-
NOT the Crown Jewels

DO NOT TOUCH THE GLASS

The Crown Jewels

MISS. DRAMATIC OSCAR-WINNING ACTRESS

totally LOST it.

And the oscar goes to...

Thief! Thief!

Someone's stolen my bracelet!

Someone's stolen my bracelet!

Thief! Thief!

Next, she gave lil' ol' innocent ME the most full-on evil eye
ever!!! Talk 2 the hand, Bianca Boticelli! i'm a thief...
NOT! Like, seriously...why would i want a bracelet
that possesses HER germs! Eeeeewwwwwwwwwwww!

✽ **Ms. Biggleton** has called an emergency sch☺☺l assembly. She has ZERO tolerance 4 stealing.

oh no, we'll miss out on our walk.

Ms.B said if the bracelet's returned 2 her office by the end of sch☺☺l 2day — NO further action will B taken. If not, the ENTIRE sch☺☺l must stay behind until the culprit owns up. Oh NO!!!!!!!!!!!!!

Like, HELLO! ...she can't B serious! (Hmmm...but is she ever not serious?...NO!) ☹ ☹ ☹ ☹ ☹ ☹ ☹ ☹ ☹ ☹

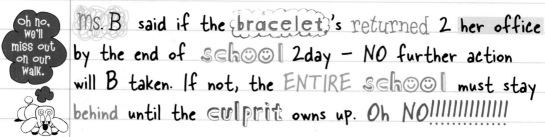

THE SERIOUS GAUGE

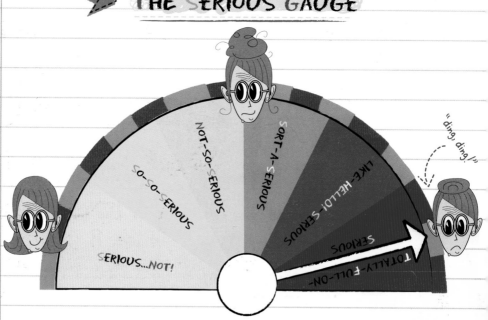

SERIOUS...NOT!

SO-SO-SERIOUS

NOT-SO-SERIOUS

SORT-A-SERIOUS

LIKE-HELLO!-SERIOUS

SERIOUS

TOTALLY-FULL-ON-SERIOUS

"ding, ding!"

After Ms. B's speech, Bianca offered a REWARD 2 any1 who finds her bracelet.

Reward = 2 ride her pony!

Like, i'd TOTALLY LOVE 2 ride a pony, but what a tragedy it's hers. i've met her pony & she's sooooooo much like Bianca — totally in LOVE with herself.

Bianca Boticelli's Bracelet is LOST

REWARD

One 15-minute ride on **Princess**, The Most Beautiful Pony Ever.

Bracelet last seen in Gym Locker Room

i love you! yes, you!

Princess

btw: a horseshoe is a good-luck charm— but the ends must B up, so the luck doesn't run out.

OH N☹☹☹☹☹☹☹!!!! Bianca Boticelli's telling EVERYONE that i STOLE HER bracelet!!! Like, she's TOTALLY spreading horrible rumors about ME.☹

How nasty!

Psst... Guess what...

mean gossiper'rer

Not-so-Perfect Bianca

Can U believe it? Yes, i know U can — like, why am i S☹☹☹☹☹☹ shocked? It's SO "typical Bianca." S'pose i assumed if i can "turn over a new leaf," so can she...but nah, not a chance, não, non, n in!!!

these R all different ways of saying "no," incl. portuguese, french & german.

OH dear!!...now everyone's totally talking 'bout ME (or so it seems)...mayB i'm just being completely paranoid???... NAH, i'm not — i just heard Pia Primrose say my name & give ME the most full-on no joke dirty l☺☺k. She couldn't B any more obvious. She's SOOOOO subtle...not

Crikey, U know i adore being the center of attention, it's my all-time favorite role — but not like this!

Miki (remember, my bEstEsT fRiEnd EVER, after **Fifi-BELLE** of course), overheard Bianca calling ME her no.1 suspect, just 'cause i was seen leaving the locker room last. But i swear, i stayed back 'cause i was daydreaming about winning ⊙WIMBLEDON⊙, U know, the world's most famous tennis competition. ...C, this always happens when i put on my tennis outfit...

Yeahhhhh! She wins again.

What a champion!

She's my hero.

Ahh...i'd like 2 thank my mum, my dad..& especially Fifi-belle, my coach...

Hmmm...just like when i put on my swimsuit — i picture myself winning the 100-meter Olympic freestyle... & i 4ever win the New York Marathon every time i slip on my runners...

how fast-lookin' R my runners!

Doesn't everyone???

So, what am i supposed 2 DO? Like, i'm sooooooooooooooo TOTALLY innocent, but the ENTIRE school, OK, slight exaggeration, MOST of them, R looking @ ME weirdly. 4 once, i swear (cross my heart), this isn't my imagination!

How can **i** prove **i** didn't steal Bianca's (bracelet)? Guess "Innocent until proven guilty" doesn't exist in **Miss.Perfect's** world?! MayB **Miki** has a suggestion?

※ ※ ※ ※ ※ ※ ※ ※ ※ ※ ※ ※

Unreal idea! **Miki**'s **Granddad** was this full-on

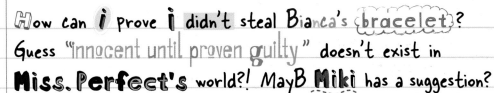
INTERNATIONAL ※ SECRET ※ SPY back in his

younger days. Recently, **Granddad Minski** has "*lost his marbles*" in a major way & spends all day babbling on about **SPY** secrets. Now **Miki** knows loads of tricks of the **SPY** trade. She says we should use these tricks 2 catch the REAL **thief** & clear my name! ☺

> But you tell ME everything.

So...Lesson 1: 2 B a **SPY**, 1 needs 2 B SecReTiVe (shhhh)...hmmm...yep, i can B that.

A **SPY** also needs 2 B cunning, intelligent & observant. ✓Check, ✓check, ✓check...that's ME 2 a tee!

Knowing many languages goes far...hmmm. Let's think, i speak *English*, **Australian**, **35** words of **French**, 2 words of **japanese** & **10** words of **Italian**. i also understand Fifi-belle... & she speaks "canine"...does that count?

A **SPY** must know sElf-dEfEnsE, B a maSter of diSguiSe & have a *desire 2 save the world.* Ahhh...i've always wanted 2 save the world!

A spy must know how 2 fly plAnes & hElicopters, parAchute, climB mountains, scuBa divE, drive sports caRs very. V. fast, reAd mAps, eScape FrOm diRe situAtioNs & rEad seCret cOdeS.

Oops, i'm failing dismally. <u>But</u> i DO have my v. own secret code!!!

Check it out: ★★★★★☆☆★★★☆★★★★★★★★★★☆☆★★★★★★★★★★

A	B	C	D	E	F	G	H	I	J	K	L	M

N	O	P	Q	R	S	T	U	V	W	X	Y	Z

Hmmm...& isn't getting in2 TROUBLE a diRe situAtioN? Every now & then i even have 2 talk my way out of it, escape a terrifying punishment! OK, so detention isn't that terrifying.

A **SPY** always needs a **partner**, a **faithful** **sidekick**. Well, no problems there... **Fifi-belle** is my constant little shadow & absolutely L♥♥♥VES a mystery. (She also looks f-a-n-t-a-b-u-l-o-u-s in a trench coat & a beret.)

(Pssssst...don't tell any1...but i actually smuggled **FIFI-BELLE** in2 sch☺☺l 2day!!! She L♥VES hanging out in my backpack & sometimes i let her out when no **teachers** R 'round. i generally do this when **Mum**'s "away on business." i can't stand Fifi being @ **HOME** alone.)

KYLA MAY

FIFI-BELLE

me & my sidekick

international super spyies

I love going to school.

shhhhhh, don't tell!

Now, Fifi...ready to help me solve a mystery? Ahh...good girl!

* **Miki** says no **SPY**'s complete without her gadgets & disguises.

So...hmmm... DiSGUiSe "must-haves".

(in other words, outfits...cool - time 4 a new wardrobe!)

some scarves...

a black, blond, red & brunette wig...

some hats...

a few mustaches...

& warm coats 4 stakeouts...

boots 4 walking...

shoes 4 stalking
(may need 2 find some
other shoes???)...

...there we go - wardrobe complete!

* GaDGeT "must-haves" *

ViDeo-suRveillAnce/
Camera SunglAsses...

Hmmm...classic Jackie-O style
with reverse telephoto lens 4 me please.

O-soooo fabuloso, Darlink!

An **international super spy** never leaves home
without **several** passports & **loads of** foreign currency.

North

West ←→ East

South

$ dollar £ pound ¢ cent ¥ yen f franc € euro

btw:
these R all
different
currency
symbols.

A **SPY** also needs a GPS watch. Global Positioning
System is this funky worldwide *navigational system*
that uses satellites (which R sort of like computers
in spaceships) in **Space** (as in, up in the sky where the
stars R) 2 locate any1 or anything @ anytime...pretty
C☺☺L, hey! (Does GUCCI make a GPS watch? Hope so!)

Do
they
suit me?

An InteRnatioNal SatelliTe
pHONe is essential, 2, miniature
of course. Hey, what if mine's hidden
in a foundation compact? Wicked!

not actual size

35:E4:S03

A **SPY** doesn't go far WITHOUT a laser cutter.
Hmmm...MayB mine could B disguised as a **lipstick!**

spy red

this end laser!

this end lippie

i ask **Miki** if i could have rocket-propelled high heels. She Cs no reason why not! {awesome!}

A parachute is also useful.
i suggest one disguised as a
French designer tote bag!
Miki luvs my creativity.
She says if her **granddad** were
still sane, he'd B v. proud!

rip cord

BEFORE

AFTER

So Would I!!

Crikey!!! i wouldn't LIKE being a REAL international super spy ...i'd absolutely L♥♥♥♥♥♥♥VE it!!!!!!!!!!!

Oh NOO! i can't believe it (well...yes i can!). Miki & i just got soooooooooooooooo caught chatting in the hallway, while everyone else had gone 2 class! The bell rang ages ago, but we were SO engrossed in conversation, we T☺TALLY didn't hear it. ☹

MAJOR OOOOPS!

oh no! oops! woopsie! in trouble again! oh deary me!

D'oh! × 100

We've BOTH been given lines...now that's a 1st!

I must always concentrate in class
I must always concentrate in class
I must always concentrate in class
I must always concentrate in class
I must always concentrate in class
I must always concentrate in class
I must always concentrate in class
I must always concentrate in class
I must always concentrate in class
I must always concentrate in class
I must always concentrate in class
I must always concentrate in class
I must always concentrate in class
I must always concentrate in class

I must always concentrate in class
I must always concentrate in class
I must always concentrate in class
I must always concentrate in class
I must always concentrate in class
I must always concentrate in class
I must always concentrate in class
I must always concentrate in class
I must always concentrate in class
I must always concentrate in class
I must always concentrate in class
I must always concentrate in class
I must always concentrate in class
I must always concentrate in class
I must always concentrate in class

It's lunchtime & **Miki**'s still distressed over her *lines*, but @ least she's talking again, much better than the incoMpreHensible baBBle i've endured 4 the past hour. Like, HELLO!...i can't remember ever NOT having *lines*. No big deal 4 ME. Miki, ♡ i know you're my bEstEsT fRiEnd & all, but get over it all right already

We've just run in2 Sienna (my 2nd bEstEsT fRiEnd) & updated her on my DRAMA. She's 110% committed 2 clearing my name — what a fRiEnd. She's, like, totally obsessed with **SPY** & DETECTIVE films!! All she wants 2 B when she grows up is a DETECTIVE. She can't wait 2 help.

Yeah! I've broken the code.

We continue 2 *formulate our* **SPY** *plan.*

& by the way, from now on some of my journal will appear in code 4 my own protection. A spy must always cover her tracks & destroy evidence that could incriminate her.

FYI:

acnaiB = enemy#1

ikiM = bstfnd#1

anneiS = bstfnd#2

anneiS says the 1st thing a **SPY** must do is devise a **mission**.

Hmmm...my  **MISSION** *(should i choose 2 accept it, which, duh, i do!)* **is:**

CONFIDENTIAL

My mission is to:
- *Find the missing bracelet*
- *Catch the thief*
- *Clear my name*
- *And be home in time for dinner*

dinner's ready!!! come & get it...

Next we must go over the crime scene with a fine-tooth comb.

Then list any SUSPECTS...hmmm...hmmm...now let's C...who doesn't like acnaiB? Like, how much TIME do we have?????????????

23

Following anneiS's suggestion, we investigate the crime scene & retrace acnaiB's footsteps...

(as made by her yucky lime-green crocodile-skin boots from Milan, **Italy**, darlink! So HOT...*NOT!*)

YUKKY wukky don't wukky (don't wukky)

anneiS wishes she was a REAL-life DETECTIVE so she could investigate the crime scene 4 forensic evidence. Hmmm...just *imagine*!

this is ikiM's ←

this is acnaiB's →

& this is my locker ↜

CRIME SCENE   DO NOT ENTER   CRIME SCENE   DO NOT ENTER   CRIME SC

CRIME SCE...   CRIME SCENE   DO NOT ENTER   CRIME SC

CRIME SCENE   DO NOT ENTER   CRIME SCENE   DO NOT ENTER   CRIME SC

But as we live in REALITY & not in our imagination (what a pity!)...we don't find ANY clues 2 solve this mystery. ☹

ohhhh... she just missed some chewing gum! Shame.

So weird... Fifi-belle's like, TOTALLY out-of-control, agitated & acting weirdo. (She must B truly feeling my anguish...hmmm, what an amazing [nonhuman] bEstEsT fRiEnd.)

She's scratching & pawing @ the locker nonstop & running 'round in circles!!!! Mmmm...perhaps she's got fleas??? ...Eeeewwww, gross!

Come on, Fifi, concentrate...U need 2 help me solve this mystery. After all, U R a DOG...U R designed 4 finding stuff.

Please! I don't have fleas.

Since we have absolutely ZERO leads, ikiM suggests we follow acnaiB over lunchtime 2 establish her behavioral pattern. We must have her *under surveillance* 2 study her EVERY move.

Hmmm...i bet she's hiding something!
MayB she concocted this whole charade 2 RUIN my name?!?

Gosh, talk 'bout B😦😦😦RING!
ZZZZZZ ZZZZZZ ZZZZZZ ZZZZZZ ZZZZZZ ZZZZZZ.
Like, all she ever does is look @ herself in the mirror a MILLION times OR admire the picture of her pony "Princess" a trillion, ZILLION times. Oh,...not 4getting time spent spreading horrible rumors 'bout ME !!! (enough, all right already!)

Hmmm...surely we're missing something? Like, WHO stole her bracelet. i know there's a simple explanation! Eek, time's running out...i'm feeeeeeeeeling TOTALLY STRESSSSSSSSSSSSSSSSSSSSSSSSSSSSSSSSSSSSSSSSSSSSSSED OUT 2 the MAX.

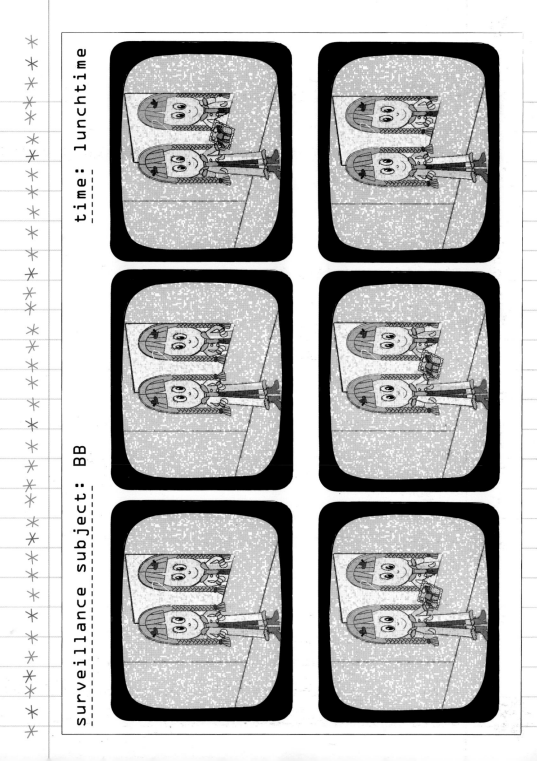

Ohhhh...like, **i SO** wish i were a REAL SPY...then i'd B able 2 clear my name. Crikey, acnaiB illecitoB would B NO match 4 KYLA MAY, **international super spy**. i could SPY on her & investigate any suspicious behavior that'd lead me 2 the perpetrator of this malicious crime.

☆ ★ ☆ ★ ☆ ★ ☆ ★ ☆ ★ ☆ ★ ☆ ★ ☆

Hmmm...just _imagine_...if i were a REAL SPY i could have a (command) (center) hidden behind a trapdoor in my sch☺☺l locker. How totally awesome would that B!

KM scanner

4 SECURITY PURPOSES 2 ENTER , i'd have a retina & fingerprint scanner, followed by a Q & A on my all-time FAVE foods.

(question & answer)

entry authorized

Her favorite foods? Chocolate & cookies.

Inside would B floor 2 ceiling major HIGH-TECH COMPUTER that capture EVERY MOVE of acnaiB...among other things. With this equipment, acnaiB wouldn't have a chance @ framing multi-talented ME!

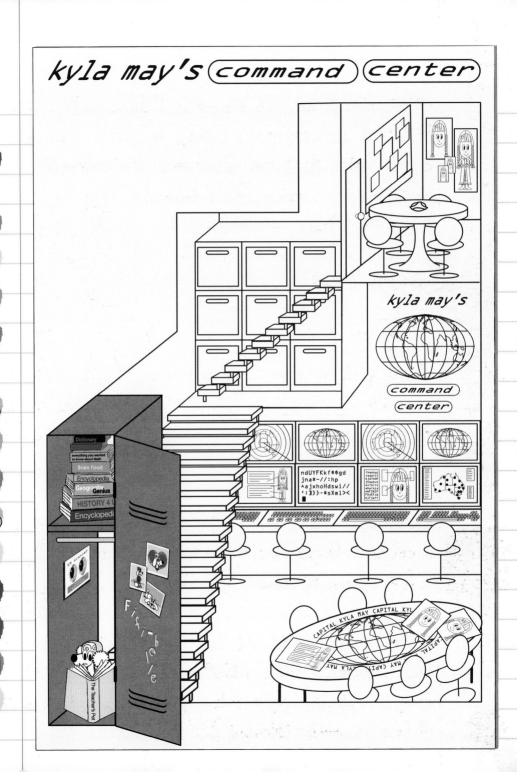

Hmmm...i could also plant a BUG on acnaiB. (wicked!!!)
D'oh, not an insect — though that'd B absolutely
HYSTERICAL! (hee hee!)...but a microscopic
listening device disguised as a hair clip 2
listen 2 her conversations.

...obviously it was Kyla May...like, who else could it have been!

Can I get some of those sunglasses, too?

Hey, mayB i could plant a Hidden Video Camera in
Gemima's sunglasses as well. (In case U don't remember,
Gemima is acnaiB's DOG...the poor thing, she must suffer from
such depression after spending so much time with Miss. BOOORING!)
The sunglasses would send images 2 my surveillance
command center.

Hmmm... IF ♡ i were a REAL SPY, just *imagine* what disguises i could wear 2 SPY on acnaiB illecitoB? MayB i'd go undercover, pRetending 2 B...

...Her pony-riding instructor?

Name:
Doris Dasher

Occupation:
BB Pony-riding Instructor

Disguise Requirements:
velvet helmet, riding outfit, saddle & whip, birthmark on ankle

Location of Interaction with Subject:
Hanging Rock Pony Club

Interaction time:
Sat @ 0800

Hmmm...

Name:
Trudy Lovegrove

Occupation:
BB Maid

Disguise Requirements:
maid's dress, apron, duster, polish, mole on chin

Location of Interaction with Subject:
Throughout Main Residence

Interaction time:
Mon-Fri @ 0600-2100

Or her maid?

Name:
James Home

Occupation:
BB Chauffeur

Disguise Requirements:
mustache, black suit, white shirt, black tie, driver's license

Location of Interaction with Subject:
The Family Limousine

Interaction time:
Mon-Fri @ 0600-2100

Her chauffeur?

Hmmm...

FOR YOUR EYES ONLY

What about her after-school Latin teacher?

Name:
Antonio Labrusca

Occupation:
BB Latin Teacher

Disguise Requirements:
pencil mustache, Italian accent, caraf, loud Italian silk shirt, long curly 1990s hair

Location of Interaction with Subject:
Main Residence Study

Interaction time:
Tues @ 1600

I have the best owner.

Or even Gemima's dog-walker?

(i still don't get WHY acnaiB can't walk her own dog, like, i'd never give up time spent with Fifi-belle!)

Name:
Jean-Luc Phillipe

Occupation:
BB Fencing Instructor

Disguise Requirements:
fencing outfit, helmet, sword, french accent, limp, scar on face, left arm & right thigh

Location of Interaction with Subject:
Main Residence Gym

Interaction time:
Wed @ 1630

Or her fencing instructor?

FOR YOUR EYES ONLY

Name:
Hilda McBottomworth

Occupation:
BB Dog-walker

Disguise Requirements:
big puffy hairdo, caftan, beads, flairs, leash, doggie-treats, nervous twitch (possibly from fleas)

Location of Interaction with Subject:
Main Residence Grounds

Interaction time:
Mon-Fri @ 1700

Hmmm...SO...if i were a real spy, i'd go undercover as the fencing instructor, 'cause his face is totally covered...& i'm pretty fabuloso @ a French accent!

Ahhhh...IF ONLY............then i'd SO B able 2 dish the dirt on acnaiB!

mum

33

✻ ✻
✻

BUT hang on, like, if **i were a 4** REAL **international super spy**, i wouldn't even NEED 2 WORRY 'bout Bianca Boticelli oops...i mean acnaiB illecitoB Like, really...i'd T☺TALLY have far, far, far **MORE IMPORTANT *missions*** 2 streSSSS over.

Hmmm...hmmm...**wow**, *imagine* if i were a proper **SPY** ....i'd travel somewhere totally interesting 2 solve a mystery !!!

Hmmm...like, mayB 2 Russia on a secret stealth jet... 2 uncover a DIAMOND smuggling ring.

Hmmm, who could i be?

My name could B " Agent Mink ," ¿ HQ (headquarters) delivers me a secret transmission in code, revealin

```
Agent Mink

We think diamonds are being smuggled
out of Moscow on dog collars.
Find the smugglers.
STOP this ring immediately.
Good luck.

HQ
```

(btw: Moscow is Russia's capital city)

A stealth jet is an invisible plane, that is, it can't B detected by radar - amazing, hey? What will they think of next?

Back here is Moscow's most famous landmark - Red Square

Agent Mink reporting for duty...

As `Agent Mink`, i'm a *world famous*, trendsetting, adventure-seeking, gadget wielding, genius-intelligent, fantabulous **super spy**, & this CASE is no challenge 4 ME & Fifi-BELLE, a.k.a. "`Agent K9`."

this is a typical Russian ha 'cause it' SOOOO col

InteRNation

Can U tell that this is really me & Fifi? Like, of course not!

Aren't i fabulous!

Hmmm...

4 this **MISSION**,
i **disguise** myself as the world-champion breeder of CHOW CHOWS. i'm competing in the "InteRNatiONaL DOG ShoW."

No one can C thru my cover as i'm awesome @ impersonations...essential 4 a SPY of MY caliber.

Isn't it funny how dog owners look like their dogs?!

Best in Show

Ohhhh, i hope we win, Fifi, oops...i mean Agent K9.

BEFORE Poodle

AFTER Chow Chow

Best in Show

Fifi-BELLE is cunningly disguised as a CHOW CHOW. (Ohhhhhhhhhhh, isn't she cute!)

in a competitive, determined, undercover-spy kinda way!

...It's day 2 of the DOG SHOW & Agent K9's made it 2 the finals. (As if we'd expect anything less!) She's, like, TOTALLY convincing the judges that she's an authentic champion CHOW CHOW.

Best in Show
- [x] Gait
- [x] Coat
- [x] Bite
- [x] Obedience
- [x] Head
- [x] Eyes
- [x] Ears
- [x] Stance

The other competitors R totally envious of Fifi's perfection as a Chow Chow.

(FIFI, U R v. cute, but i much prefer U as a poodle.)

International Dog Show

So far, NOTHING stands out??? We've yet 2 C a DOG with a --DIAMOND-- collar. How weird! This case isn't so easy. (But then who ever said that being an international super spy would B easy?)

Instead, we notice plenty of...

Hmmm... no BLING so far.

FUR

SEQUINS

Hey! That dog has fleas.

TARTAN

& SATIN.

Hmmm...MayB HQ got it wrong???

But...wait a minute...what's that??? In the distance i C a SPARKLE! The glint is coming from the collar of Petra, the "Best in Show" Pekingese.

Her breeder hardly looks like the smuggler type, but i've learned as an international super spy 2 never judge a book by its cover...in this case...outfit.

Check out her BLING!

Ok, i'm feeling good about my hunch, but i need some hard evidence B4 i can make my (impressive, even by SPY standards) move.

ME & Fifi-belle, Oops, i mean Agent K9 & i pursue the Pekingese & her breeder as they leave the Dog Show. Agent K9 follows their scent 2 make sure we're on the right track.

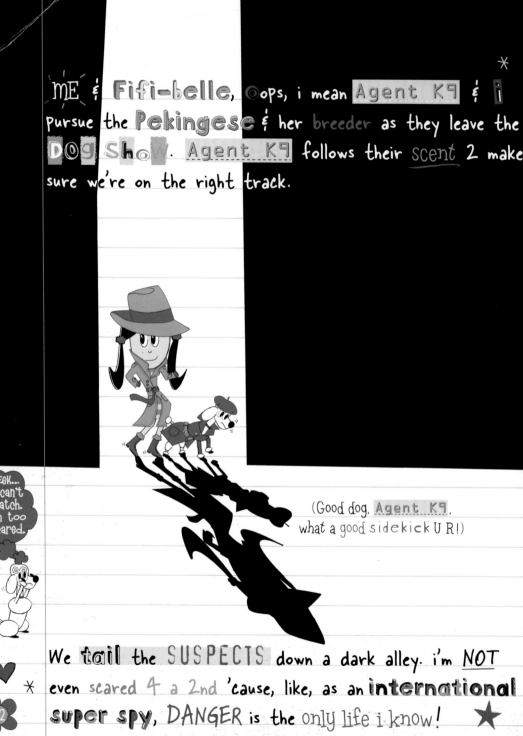

Eek...
I can't
watch.
I'm too
scared.

(Good dog, Agent K9, what a good sidekick U R!)

We tail the SUSPECTS down a dark alley. i'm NOT even scared 4 a 2nd 'cause, like, as an international super spy, DANGER is the only life i know!

Up ahead A mysterious black car pulls in2 the shadows. S—L—O—W—L—Y...the car door opens... a tall stranger steps out of the car & starts talking in Russian 2 the Pekingese breeder.

We can't hear a thing! Even though we're fluent in Russian, the suspects R 2 far away 2 B heard.

The suspects exchange briefcases. Agent K9 creeps closer with a super-sonic audio-capture micro-chip phone. No **MISSION** is 2 big 4 my trusty partner.

I'm very creepy!

creep   creep   creep

As they open the leather cases, i use my infraRED night-vision goggles 2 reveal the contents – MONEY in 1, DIAMONDS in the other! Hooray!!!! ☺

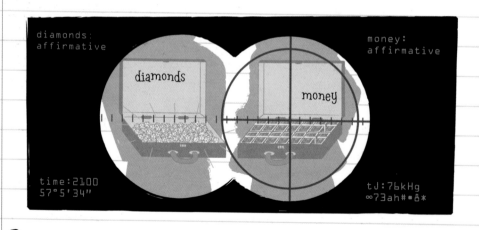

diamonds:
affirmative

diamonds

money:
affirmative

money

time:2100
57°5'34"

tJ:76kHg
∞73ah#•8*

But no time 2 celebrate yet. Our **MISSION** is FAR from over. We may have our evidence, but now the real danger begins – we must CAPTURE these crooks.

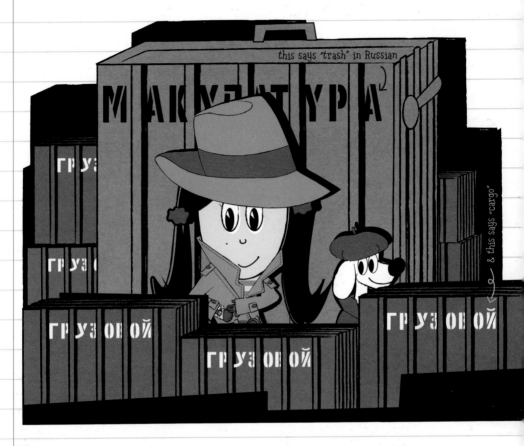

i quickly send a `coded message` 2 **HQ** using my
G.P.S. satellite communicator
(**disguised** as a v. stylish *designer* watch).
i request immediate **backup** – not 'cause `Agent K9`
& i can't handle these villains on our own, but due 2
international super spy protocol, or as we
like 2 call it in the business: R.E.S.P.E.C.T. 2 **HQ**.

Agent K9 races 2 BLOCK the other end of the alley, while i overcome the thieves with a routine of KICKBOXING, KARATE CHOPS & KUNG FU (moves i studied @ Spy Academy where i majored in Eastern methods of self-defense).

Ha!!! They never saw ME coming! Wit 2nds i have 'em pinned 2 the ground. C, this is WHY i AM the bEstEsT international super spy EVERRRRRRRRR!

Oh, & don't worry, *no animals* were harmed in the making of this ARREST. `Agent K9` cornered `Petra`, the **Pekingese**. Once she saw **Fifi's** fine canine stature, she rolled over on2 her back in TOTAL submission.

Grrrrrrr...

eek!

Chow Chow for now!

Just as BACKUP ARRIVES, i `Agent Mink` open the car trunk, revealing a trunk full of ⟶DIAMONDS⟵. Unreal!!!! CASE SOLVED!

☺ ☺

Riiiinnnngggg Ring. Oops...back 2 **reality** (shame – i so much prefer my *imagination*)! The bell's ringing, which means *English class is* over. i SO can't *believe* i didn't get caught daydreaming then Like, how T☺TALLY lucky am i? The last thing i need 2day is detention as well.

Oh NO!!! i only have a few hours left 2 clear my name, & ikiM, anneiS & i R NO closer 2 solving this mystery. Like, how unfair is life? ☹

anneiS suggests we try 2 piece 2gether our crime scene investigation. Hmmm...we still don't have any suspects. Or a motive. Apart from the well-known fact acnaiB's just mean

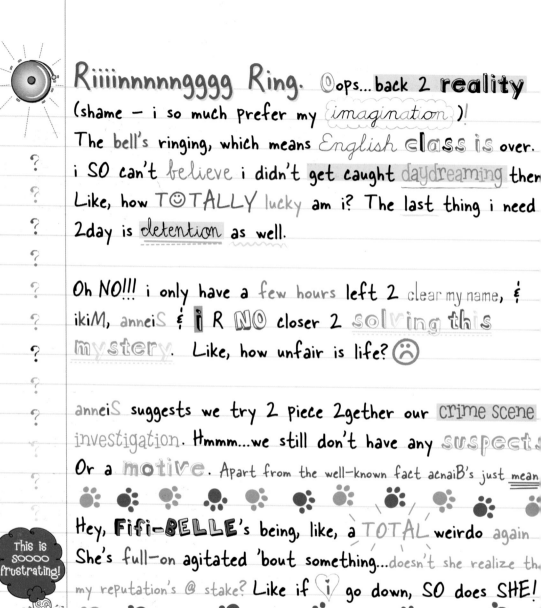

Hey, **Fifi-BELLE**'s being, like, a TOTAL weirdo again She's full-on agitated 'bout something...doesn't she realize the my reputation's @ stake? Like if ♡i go down, SO does SHE!

Fifi, we don't have time 4 this! Like, i'm totally BuSY @ the moment...the clock's ticking...

mental note: check **FIFI-BELLE** 4 fleas.

This is soooo frustrating!

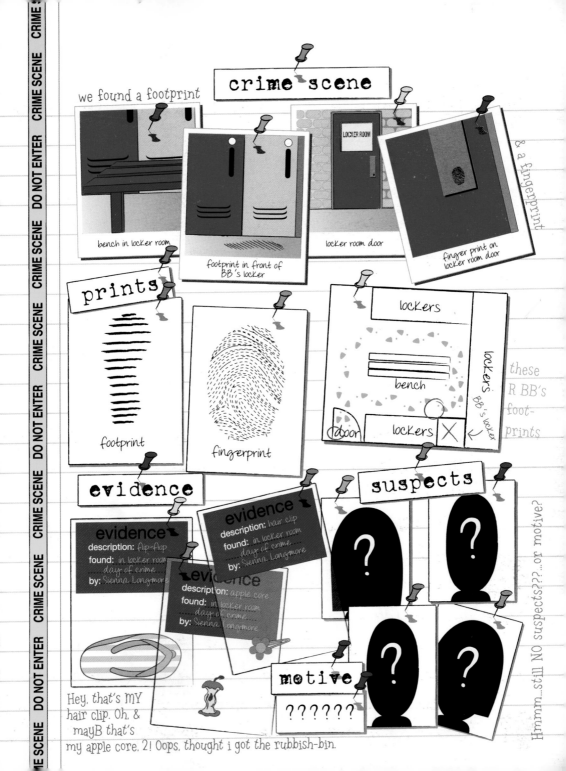

crime scene

we found a footprint

bench in locker room

LOCKER ROOM

footprint in front of BB's locker

locker room door

& a fingerprint

finger print on locker room door

prints

footprint

fingerprint

lockers

bench

door

lockers

lockers BB's locker

these R BB's foot-prints

evidence

evidence
description: flip-flop
found: in locker room day of crime
by: Sienna Longmore

evidence
description: hair clip
found: in locker room day of crime
by: Sienna Longmore

evidence
description: apple core
found: in locker room day of crime
by: Sienna Longmore

suspects

? ? ? ?

motive

??????

Hey, that's MY hair clip. Oh, & mayB that's my apple core, 2! Oops, thought i got the rubbish-bin.

Hmmm...still NO suspects???...or motive?

Scrap the crime scene — ikiM has a NEW plan.
We'll go undercover & follow acnaiB during afternoon
break. What a TOTALLY awesome idea!
(Shame it wasn't mine!)

14:00: Nothing 2 report... (btw: a REAL SPY only ever
uses the 24-hour clock.)

14:05: Still nothing 2 report (Zzzz Zzzz Zzzz).

14:10: Reporting that i can't stop yawning...
in fact even my yawns R yawning.

14:15: Anyone got some matchsticks? I can no
longer keep my eyes open.

14:20: Reporting i am officially asleep...
Wake me if necessary.

14:25: Ahh something 2 report at last: acnaiB's
father is here — wonder why? We overhear him
saying 2 acnaiB "your mother's sent me to school
because you left your homework at home.
Darling, you're always misplacing things."

50

Oh dear — the bell's ringing. Back 2 **class** we go.

This is **terrible!** i feel like the WHOLE school's against ME, well @ least 1/2, all right. How CAN they believe acnaiB? Just proves what **nasty gossip** can do.

There's only a couple of hours left B4 **Ms. Biggleton**'s deadline.

i can't bear 2 shoulder this BURDEN. ☹

i want 2 run away, change schools, suburbs?, ...even countries! MayB i could start a new life!

That'll B soooooooooooooooooooooooooooooo much easier.

Hmmm...if i move countries, where could i live?

Mmmm....what about Greenland?

I thought Greenland would be green.

Brrrrr...222 ccoollldddd!

Hmmm...mayB Hawaii, USA?

"Aloha" means "hello" & "good-bye" in Hawaiian.

Aloha Hawaii

After all, i AM the bEstEsT
HULA DANCER EVER.

& i could SURF! COOL, DUUUDE.

Hmmm...mayB **NEPAL**, so NO ONE could EVER find ME? Wicked!

Heaps of people go 2 Nepal 2 hike 'cause it has the biggest mountains ever. Kathmandu is the capital city.

Oh...but Fifi & i would B oh so lonely.

i really need warm weather...so mayB i'll escape 2 th **Sahara Desert** in **Africa**?

Oh, I'm so thirsty.

No way José...way 2 hot. ☹

What about  where my grandparents live?

that's my Dad's mum & dad. i'm Australian, but they're English.

i could B a guard @ the Queen of England's place - U know, Buckingham Palace.

As a London Guard U R never allowed 2 smile?...Hmmm, this may B difficult.

Cool...this is unreal - no one will ever find me under this hat! Fifi, you're not smiling, R U?

Like...HELLO!...brilliant idea YAM ALYK.

Ohhh...but it rains a lot in the UK

MayB it'd B easier 2 run away somewhere in Australia. Hmmm...now, where could i live if i couldn' live here?

Hmmm...what about Queensland? It's sooooooooooo gorgeous & hot up there. i could swim with the dolphins aaaaaaaaaaaalllllllll day long. TOTALLY funky

Byron is a beautiful coastal town in northern New South Wales where we vacation.

Or i could B a hippie in **BYRON BAY,** chilling out, man, doing yoga?

Humm mmmm mmm mmmm mmm...

Hummmmmmmmmmmmmmmmmmmmmmmmmmmmmmmmm
Hummmmmmmmmmmmmmmmmmmmmmmmmmmmmmm
Hummmmmmmmmmmmmmmmmmmmmmmmmmmmmm
Hummmmmmmmmmmmmmmmmmmmmmmmmmmmm
Hummmmmmmmmmmmmmmmmmmmmmmmmmmm
Hummmmmmmmmmmmmmmmmmmmmmmmmmm
Hummmmmmmmmmmmmmmmmmmmmmmmmm
Hummmmmmmmmmmmmmmmmmmmmmmmm

Oh, life would B SOOOO much easier if i could just run away from this gray cloud of accusation.

But **Mum** & **Dad** have always taught ME 2 never run from life's challenges.

i must B **TOUGH** & stand up 4 myself.

So come on, **YAM ALYK**...get O-V-E-R i-t, all right already!...hold your head up high & face this challenge head on...

57

Speaking of heads, mine's absolutely throbbing...
sch☺☺l's over & everyone's getting ready 4
final assembly. There's agony in the air. Everyone's dreadin
2 stay back. ☹

ikiM thinks we have just enough time 2 race back 2 the
crime scene. She feels we're missing something.
We rush thru the crowd.

Frustratingly, we still can't C anything. ☹ ☹ ☹

Fifi-BELLE's T☺TALLY hysterical now.
She's nonstop scratching & pawing @ the locker.
i've checked; she doesn't have fleas...
What's wrong, Fifi? Stop that!

Oh no, NOW she's, like, gone absolutely MAD! She's
trying 2 dig a HOLE in acnaiB's locker!!!

Yeah, finally!

Hang on - what's this? There's
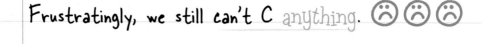
something caught in the gap???

Oh my GOSH!

...it's THE

bracelet!

That means it was NEVER STOLEN in the 1st place!

Phew!||||||||||||||||||||||||||||||||||||||||||||||||||||||

acnaiB must have misplaced it!

i can't believe it!|||||||||||||||||||||||||

i'm, like, **totally,**

absolutely

furious.

i don't have the ability 2 use colored pens & pencils — i'm 2 upset!!!!!

Oh NO!!!!!!!!!!!
. . . .

Look @ the time — it's 2:55 pm, oops i mean 14:55.
That means only 5 minutes till assembly...eek!

Quick...

RUN!!!!
. . . .

Oh my gosh...will we make it in time?
We need 2 B there A.S.A.P. Hmmm...IF ONLY we were
REAL SPIES...we could fly super-sonic mini-helicopter
& make it 2 assembly in MILLISECONDS!

Sorry...don't have time 2 draw what's in my imagination, so you're just gonna have 2 use yours instead & imagine ikiM, anneiS & i flying these really cool high-tech mini-helicopters over our school & landing outside the assembly hall. Students look up in absolute shock. & Fifi has her own smaller doggie version, like of course!

...Since we're NOT (isn't life SO boring?),
LET'S RUN AS FAST AS WE CAN!
RUUUUUUUUUUUUUUUUUUUUUUUUUUNNNNNNNNNNNNNNN...

As we run up 2 the *assembly stage* where Ms. Biggleton is already waiting, everyone's whispering "i heard it was Kyla May." It's as if they're expecting me 2 confess...like... WHAtEVEr!

We tell Ms.B EVERYTHiNG!!! She is horrified. (Pheeeeeeewwwwwwww, i'm off the hook!)

With a v. STERN look, she calls acnaiB up on *stage.* Miss. Drama Queen is SOOOOO smug on the account of convincing so many i'm T☺TALLY guilty.

Ms. Biggleton announces the bracelet has been found – the room EXPLODES with cheers; everyone can go home. & then 2 the crowd's amazement, Ms.B explains that the bracelet was NEVER STOLEN just MISPLACED!

Now it's acnaiB's turn 2 B the center of attention!! ...EVeRYoNE stares as she turns a lovely shade of crimson. Ms. Biggleton reprimands Miss.Beetroot 4 jumping 2 conclusions & spreading nasty rumors. ☺

Now that I'm in the clear, i can use proper names again.

Miki, Sienna & ♥i R commended 4 uncovering the TRUTH...& the sch☺☺l gets a lecture on honesty & being innocent until proven guilty.

Yippee...WE found the (bracelet), my name is cleared... Bianca's is smeared!...& we'll all B **HOME** in time 4 tea.

WICKED & fantAbulous × ∞ !!!!!!!!! ☺

mission completed.
Agent Mink

Hmmm...mayB we should B professional super spies when we grow up. What a brilliant idea!

The End.

FIFI-BELLE'S ANGELS

KYLA MAY's Dictionary:

2	=	to/too
2day	=	today
2morrow	=	tomorrow
2nite	=	tonight
4	=	for
4ever	=	forever
4get	=	forget
B	=	be
B4	=	before
btw.	=	by the way
C	=	see
fantabulous	=	fantastic + fabulous
in2	=	into
mayB	=	maybe
R	=	are
there4	=	therefore
U	=	you
V.	=	very
@	=	at
&	=	and
=	=	equals

A.S.A.P = as soon as Possible

Any1 = anyone

4getting = forgetting

on2 = on to

1st = first
2nd = second

1/2 = half

i give U permission 2 use my dictionary with your friends!

64